The Adventures of Paddington™

The Crown Jewels Caper

HarperCollins Children's Books

Dear Aunt Lucy,

Thank you so much for my
birthday card. I've put it pride of
place next to my bed!
I've had the **most** memorable day.
It all started with a song . . .

This book belongs to:

....

Based on the episode "Paddington and the Tower of London: parts one and two" by James Lamont and Jon Foster

Adapted by Lauren Holowaty

First published in the United Kingdom by HarperCollins *Children's Books* in 2023
HarperCollins *Children's Books* is a division of HarperCollins*Publishers* Ltd
1 London Bridge Street
London SE1 9GF

www.harpercollins.co.uk

HarperCollins*Publishers*
Macken House, 39/40 Mayor Street Upper
Dublin 1, D01 C9W8, Ireland

1 3 5 7 9 10 8 6 4 2

ISBN: 978-0-00-856811-5

Printed in the United Kingdom

Based on the Paddington novels written and created by Michael Bond

FSC™ C007454

This book is produced from independently certified FSC™ paper
to ensure responsible forest management.

For more information visit: www.harpercollins.co.uk/green

"*Happy birthday, dear Paddington . . .*"
sang the Browns, "*happy birthday to you!*"

"Oh, thank you!" said Paddington.

He blew out the candles with a *pfffft!* and made a wish.

"What did you wish for?" asked Judy.

"I wished for a wonderful birthday and here I am having one!"

Paddington handed gifts to everyone. "In Peru, we *give* presents on our birthdays," he explained.

"We have presents for you too, Paddington," said
Mr Brown, in between mouthfuls of cake. "But there
isn't time to open them as we need to go now, or
we'll miss your special birthday treat!"

Outside, Mr Brown showed Paddington the special treat – it was Bessie, his birthday tour bus!

"Would you like to go on a **London sightseeing trip?**" Mr Brown asked.

"Very much indeed!" said Paddington.

Paddington hurried back inside, placed the last slice of birthday cake under his hat and off they went!

There was so much to see in London!

Paddington gasped as they passed the Houses of Parliament. "Goodness! What an enormous clock."

Judy explained that the clock's bell was called **Big Ben.**

"Hello, Ben!" called Paddington.

DONG!

"Oh, he said 'hello' back!" said Paddington.

"Now," said Mrs Brown. "Who wants to go on a boat trip along the River Thames?"

"Me! Me! Me! Yes, please!"
they all cheered.

The Browns got on the tour boat, but just as Paddington ran to join them there was a great gust of wind – **WHOOSH!** – and his hat flew off. As he went back to get it, he heard . . . **HONK!**

"Oh no," cried Paddington. "The boat!"

"STOP! Come back!" Paddington shouted. But it was too late! Paddington watched sadly as the boat left without him.

He was wondering what to do when he spotted a rowing boat attached to the jetty. He put on a life jacket and jumped in.

Paddington had never rowed before and at first he went round in circles. Just as he got the hang of it, he got excited and let go of the oars . . .

"Oh dear," he said, as they floated away.

How was he going to catch up with the Browns now?

Suddenly a huge passing boat made a giant wave, sending Paddington spinning through a mysterious archway . . .

SPLOSH! CRASH! BANG!

The poor soggy bear found himself washed ashore in a strange place that looked a bit like a castle.

"Welcome to Traitors' Gate," said a talking sign. "Only the world's **worst criminals** arrive through *this* gate."

Well, that's not very nice! thought Paddington.

After a bit of exploring, Paddington found some nice dry clothes in a cupboard. He hung his wet ones up to dry and put the slice of birthday cake under his new hat. He looked very smart!

Back on the river, the Browns suddenly realised Paddington wasn't on board.

"I can't believe we've lost Paddington on his birthday!" cried Jonathan.

"Don't worry," said Mrs Bird. "We'll find him."

And they leaped back in Bessie to search the streets of London.

Meanwhile, Paddington bumped into someone wearing the same clothes as him.

"You must be the new Beefeater," said the man. "Welcome to the Tower of London!"

"Oh, I'm not a Beefeater," said Paddington. "I'm just lost."

"Don't worry, I'll show you around," said the Beefeater.

In the courtyard, a flock of ravens was squawking hungrily.

"Legend has it that if ever the ravens should leave the Tower of London, the city will fall," said the man.

"Well, we can't have that," said Paddington, and he was about to offer the birds some cake when the man told him it wasn't allowed.

"Oh, my mistake," said Paddington, trying to shoo them away. But the ravens started to chase him . . .

Paddington ran into a dark room to escape the hungry ravens. It was full of glittering golden objects.

"Welcome to the crown jewels," said a loudspeaker. "The most famous jewels in the entire world!"

"Wow!" said Paddington.

As Paddington looked around in wonder, he accidentally tripped and his cake flew across the room, landing SPLAT! on a crown.

"Oops!" said Paddington.

Paddington tried hooking the crown with his staff so he could clean the cake off, but as soon as he lifted it . . .

BLURRRT! BLURRRT!

. . . alarms rang, lights flashed and the Beefeater charged in, looking furious.

"WHAT'S GOING ON IN HERE?" he shouted.

"There's been a terrible mistake," Paddington tried to explain, as the conveyor belt sent him flying out the door with the crown zooming after him and landing **THUMP!** on his head!

"Come back here with **the crown jewels!**" the Beefeater shouted.

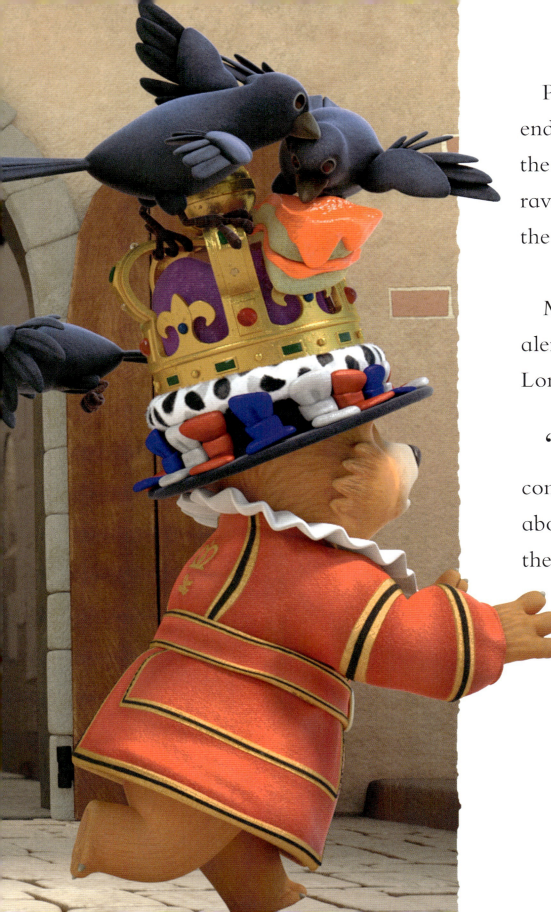

Paddington's troubles didn't end there. He was chased around the courtyard by the hungry ravens who were trying to eat the cake on the crown!

Meanwhile, the Beefeater alerted every police officer in London to the theft.

"STOP, thief!" he commanded, and he was just about to throw Paddington into the dungeon when . . .

BEEP!
BEEP!

. . . the Browns arrived with PC Wells who had heard the alert on his radio. They were very surprised to see Paddington wearing the crown and a Beefeater outfit.

Paddington explained what happened.

"Paddington is a very kind bear," PC Wells told the Beefeater. "If he says it's a mix-up, then it is."

Paddington thanked PC Wells and then ended his birthday perfectly – on a proper tour of the Tower of London with the Brown family.

It was just about the best birthday I could've hoped for, Aunt Lucy.
I saw lots of London, met a Beefeater and stopped the crown
jewels being stolen . . . by me.
I'd love to show you the Tower of London one day, but perhaps
we'll use the front door next time.

Love from,
Paddington